Written by Charles Boyle
Illustrated by Everett Davidson

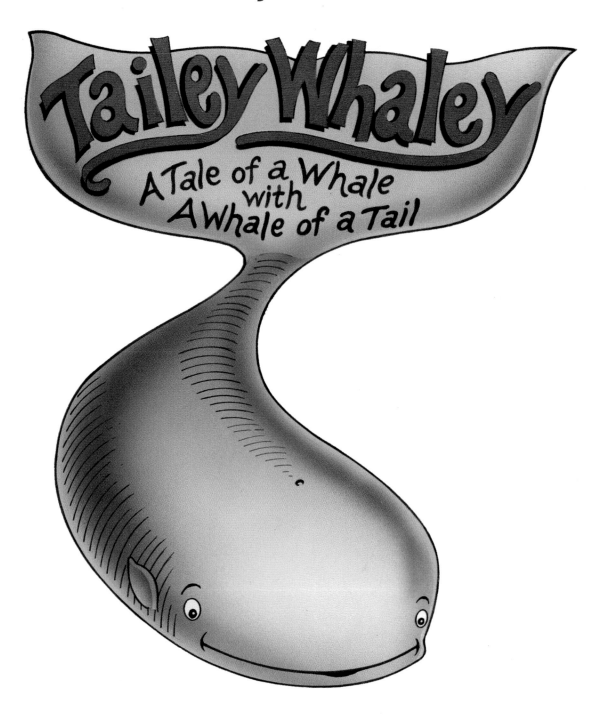

Tailey Whaley
A Tale of a Whale
with
A Whale of a Tail

Book Design by Carol Ladd

This book belongs to

_____

Name

_____

Date

Kailey was a happy whale...
her baby was ready to be born!
It had grown bigger and bigger within
her for 16 long months!

Kailey's baby was born cozy and comfortable in the warm southern ocean. The calf was a beautiful baby boy.

One of Kailey's friends noticed something. "Why, he has no tail!" she cried.

Another said, "How will he swim up for air?"

"He'll drown if he can't get air," thought Kailey. "I must *do* something to save him!"

Oh, no!

Acting quickly, Kailey used her tail to flip her baby to the surface where he could breathe.

Everyone rushed up to see if he was OK. They spotted him a long way up in the sky.

"Oh, my!" said one. "Kailey was so excited she flipped him too far!"

All of a sudden the baby's end puffed up. Then it began to unfold! "Wow! What's happening?" yelled one whale.

"It's a tail!" whooped another. "He really has a tail!"

And Kailey said, "Imagine that! He was born all wrapped up in his own tail."

Everyone cheered! Now he would be able to swim, and dive, and stay alive.

The baby's tail kept unfolding and unfolding, getting bigger and bigger and bigger. It was HUGE!

All the whales were astounded. Their jaws dropped, and their eyes popped. "I can't believe what I'm seeing!" whispered one whale.

Suddenly, Kailey realized her baby was in a new kind of danger. He was going to crash into the sea. "Oh, no!" she cried. "He's falling so fast he'll be hurt when he hits the water."

All the others held their breath. They were sure Kailey was right.

But the little whale did not crash!

Instead, he used his tail as a giant wing, did a loop-the-loop, and glided down like a bird while everybody watched in stunned silence.

The little whale flew in like a seaplane to a graceful landing.

Not even the older whales had ever seen such a huge tail! Although they were dazed and amazed, they were happy to have this special new baby join their pod.

But all the little whales laughed at the baby because he was so different. "Real whales don't fly!" sneered the meanest bully.

"Hey kid!" taunted another. "Is that your father's tail you're wearing?"

"You've sure got a whale of a tail!" snickered a third brat.

And they all hooted at him, "Tail, Tail, Tailey Whaley! Tailey Whaley! That's your name!"

Disobeying their parents, they made fun of him.
They followed him around all day, laughing at
him, and taunting him, and making him cry.

Tailey felt sad and rejected all day and all night. His mother tried to comfort him, but nothing she did or said made him feel better.

Finally, it hurt too much to stay.

So Kailey decided to swim far away and raise her baby where no one could make fun of him.

She loved everything about him, especially his great big tail. It was so beautiful to her that she decided she would call him Tailey, too!

Many years passed by as Kailey taught her youngster all she knew about life in the ocean. And Tailey taught his mom about things he learned when he went flying.

Tailey Whaley grew up smart and strong.

He was also brave. Once he fought off a whole pod of killer whales who tried to bite Kailey. He knocked them silly with his powerful tail.

One day, Tailey and his mother heard cries of fear from some whales in the distance.

Soon, they saw it was the same pod of whales they had left so long ago.

The whales were being chased by hunters from a whaling ship. One of the hunters in a fast boat was shooting harpoons at them from a big gun.

19

The whales recognized
Tailey by his big tail.
They rushed over.

"Help us!" they cried.
"Help us, Tailey Whaley!"

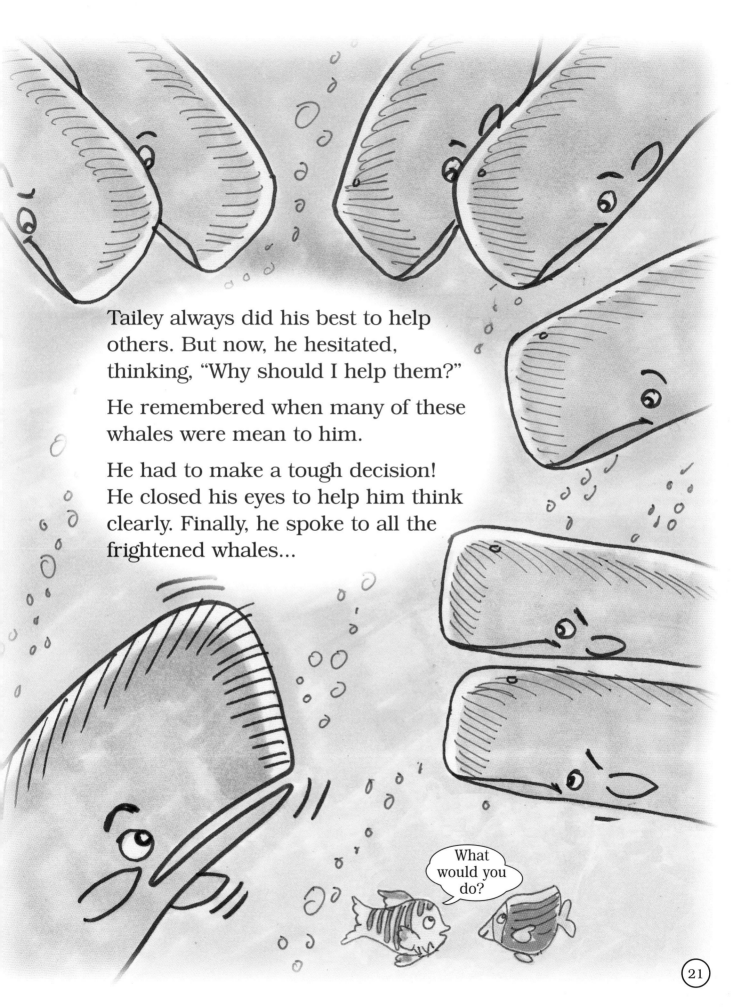

Tailey always did his best to help others. But now, he hesitated, thinking, "Why should I help them?"

He remembered when many of these whales were mean to him.

He had to make a tough decision! He closed his eyes to help him think clearly. Finally, he spoke to all the frightened whales...

What would you do?

"OK," he said, "I will try to help you."

But, right away, he realized he didn't know what to do. So, he thought hard about everything Kailey had taught him
 and
  he got some ideas
   and
    he made a plan
     and
      he swam into action.

First, Tailey Whaley
slapped the rudder
off the harpoon boat.
Now that dangerous
boat was helpless!
It could not steer.

Next, flying under his wing-tail, he butted
the terrible harpoon gun right off the bow of
the whale hunters' boat.

Then, he decided to spare the big ship
so it could take the whale hunters home.

The danger was over, so Tailey and
Kailey swam quietly away.

When the whale hunters saw that Tailey did not intend to harm them, they were puzzled.

"We were ready to hurt him," they agreed, "but he didn't even try to hurt us."

Meanwhile, the excited whales raced to catch up.

"Thank you for saving us, Tailey Whaley! We want to be your friends! Please stay with us."

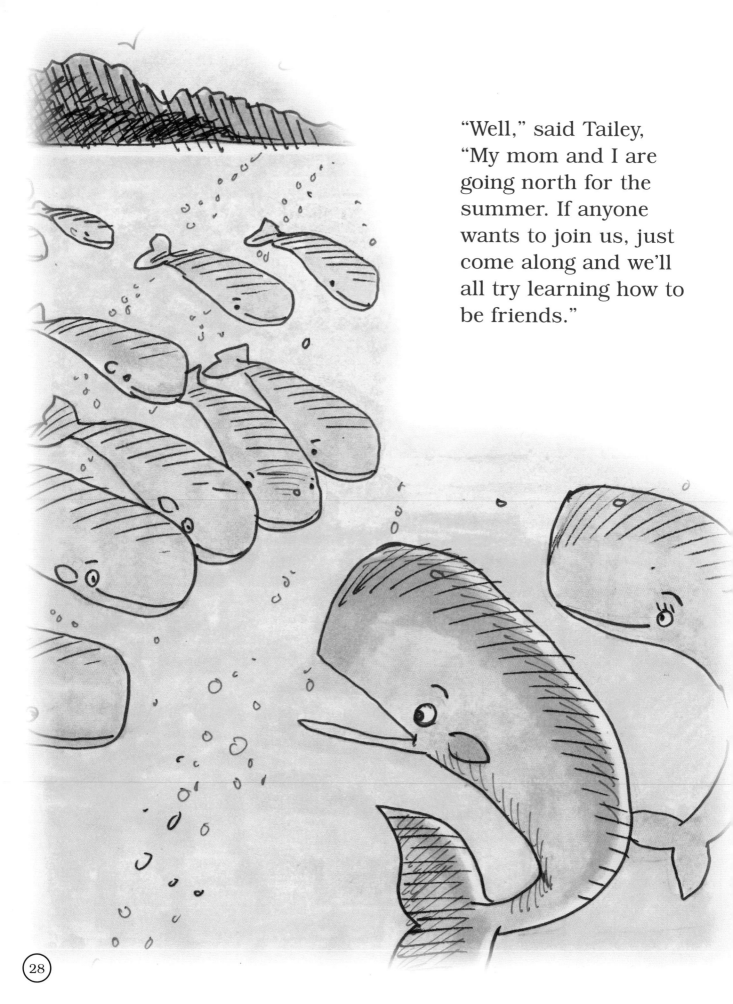

"Well," said Tailey, "My mom and I are going north for the summer. If anyone wants to join us, just come along and we'll all try learning how to be friends."

So... all the whales followed them to a secret and safe place Kailey knew.

That summer, they all learned to play and explore and work together.

And every whale who made a new friend learned what all friends know...

Now, what could that be?

EVERY FRIEND IS DIFFERENT!

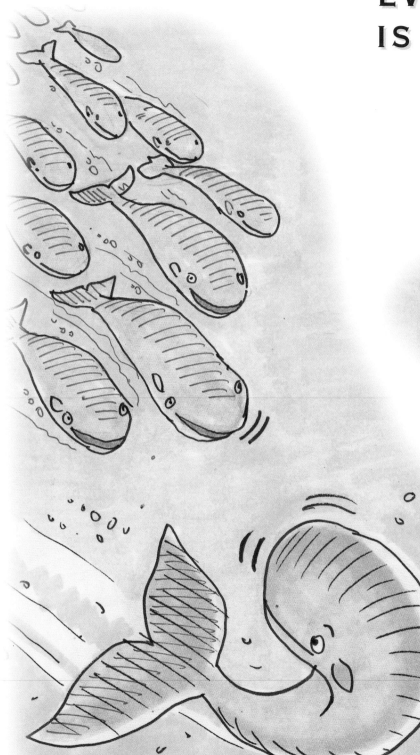

If you just take time to look, you'll see what's special.

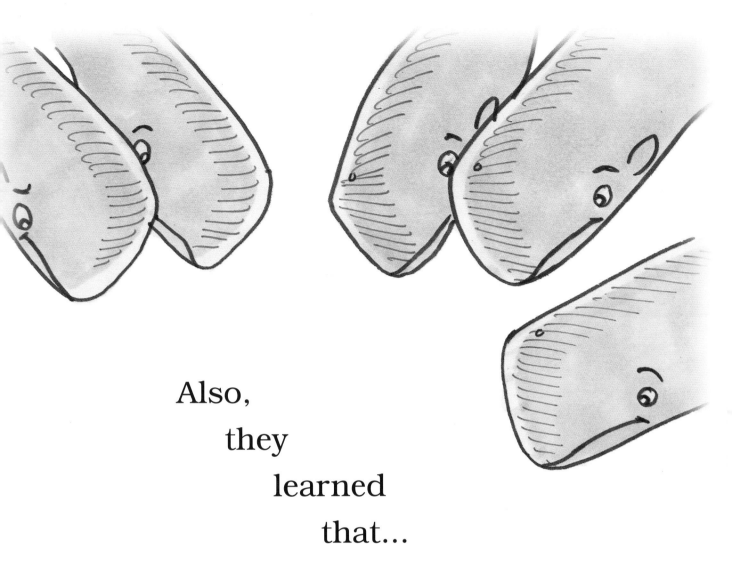

Also,
  they
    learned
      that...

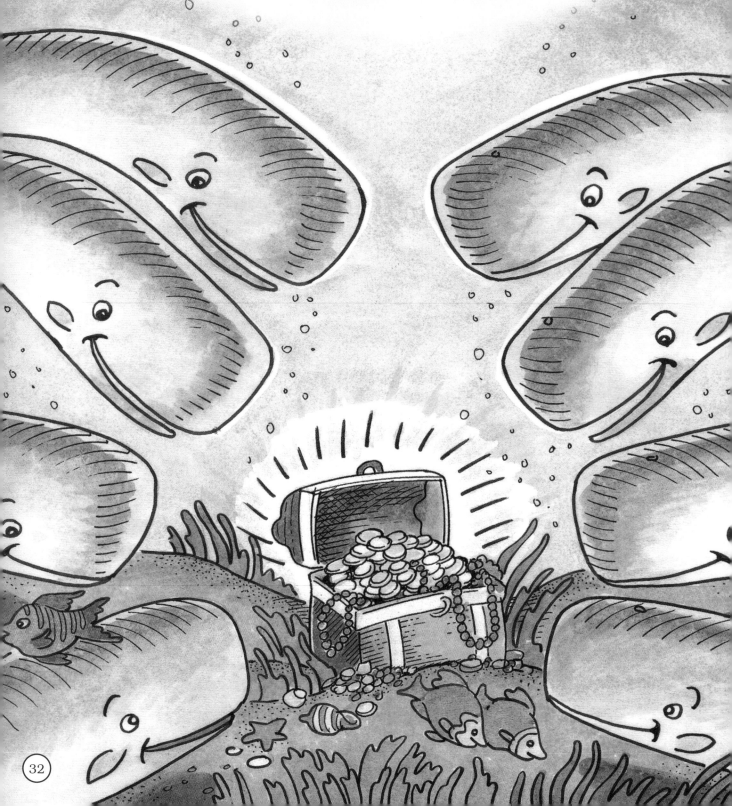
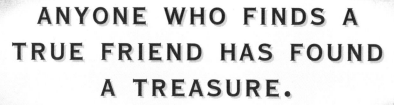

MY TREASURED FRIENDS

TAILEY

KAILEY

MY TREASURED FRIENDS

_____   _____

_____   _____

_____   _____

_____   _____

_____   _____

_____   _____

_____   _____

_____   _____

_____   _____

_____   _____